BIG BAD BUBBLE

BIG BAD BUBBLE

WORDS BY

Adam Rubin

PICTURES BY

Daniel Salmieri

HOUGHTON MIFFLIN HARCOURT   BOSTON   NEW YORK

For information about permission to reproduce
selections from this book, write to
trade.permissions@hmhco.com or to
Permissions, Houghton Mifflin Harcourt
Publishing Company, 3 Park Avenue,
19th Floor, New York, New York 10016.

www.hmhco.com
The illustrations were executed in
watercolor, pen and ink, and collage.
The text was set in 15-point Bryant.
Book design by Kerry Martin
The Library of Congress has cataloged the
hardcover edition as follows:
Rubin, Adam, 1983–
Big bad bubble/by Adam Rubin; illustrated by
Adam Salmieri.
p. cm.
Summary: With gentle prodding from the narrator
and help from the reader, four monsters are led to
face their greatest fear—bubbles.
[1. Bubbles—Fiction. 2. Fear—Fiction. 3. Monsters—
Fiction. 4. Humorous stories.] I. Salmieri, Daniel,
1983– illustrator. II Title.
PZ7.R83116Big 2014
[E]—dc23
2013020243
ISBN: 978-0-544-04549-1 hardcover
ISBN: 978-0-544-92782-7 paperback

Manufactured in China
SCP 10 9 8 7 6 5 4 3 2 1
4500642363

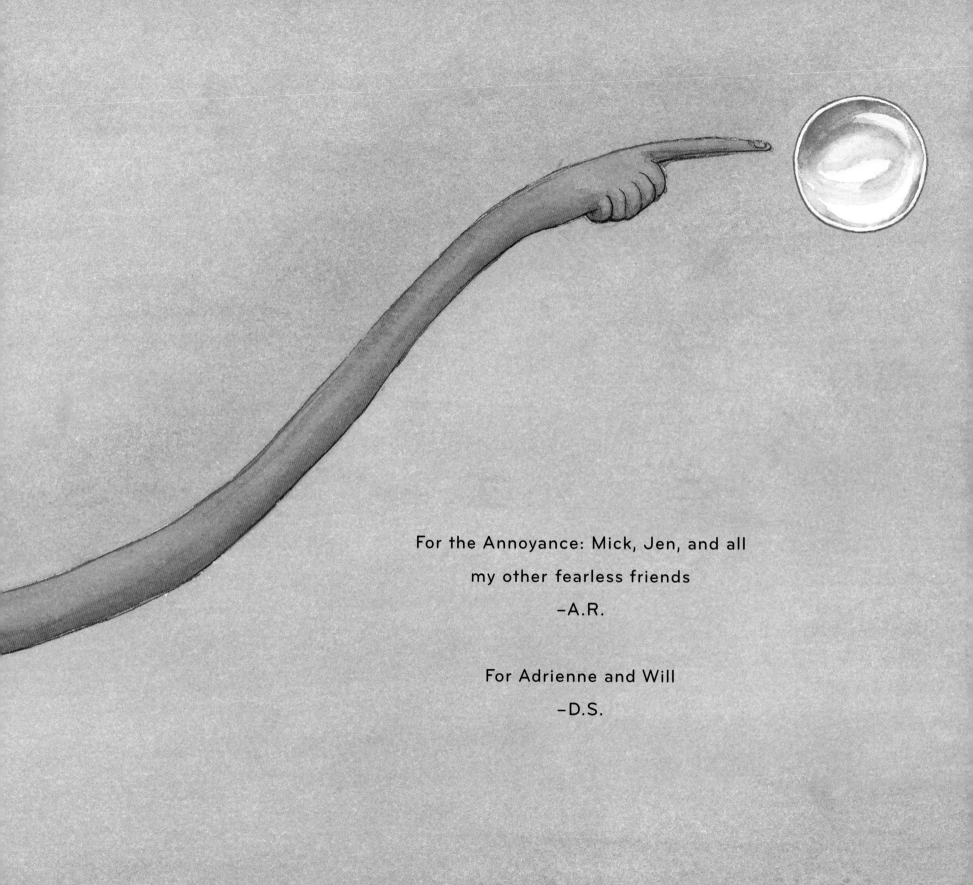

For the Annoyance: Mick, Jen, and all
my other fearless friends
—A.R.

For Adrienne and Will
—D.S.

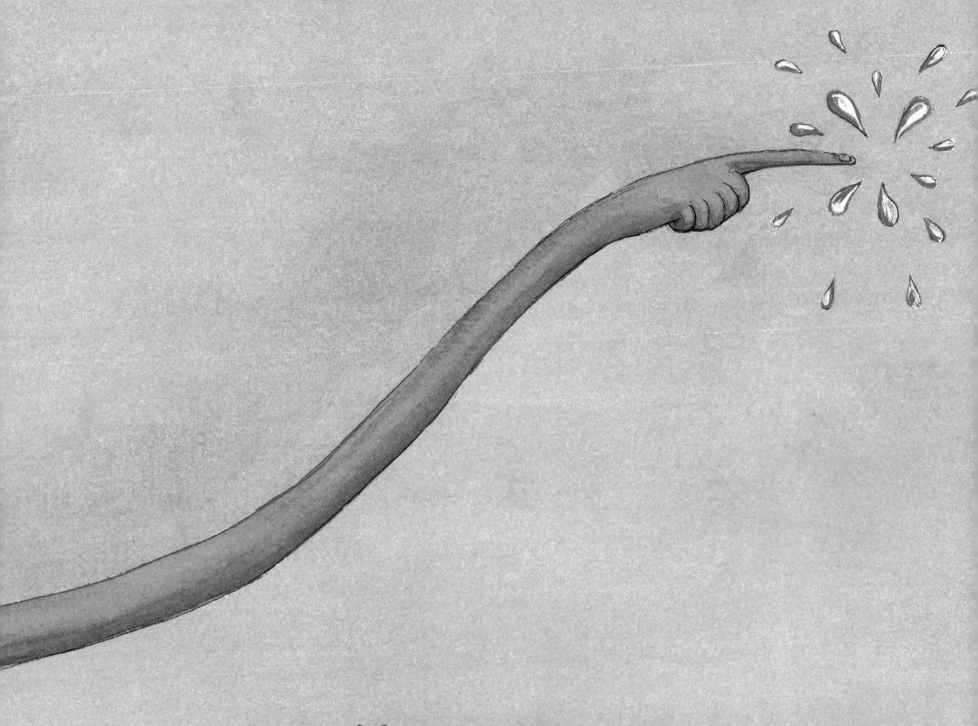

YOU may not know this, but when a bubble pops, it doesn't just disappear.

It reappears in La La Land . . .
where the monsters live.

For some reason, all the big, scary monsters are terrified of bubbles.

Froofle, why are you running away?

Yerburt, what's the matter?

Wumpus, stop crying.
(Tell Wumpus to stop crying.)

Turns out, it's all Mogo's fault. When he was little, a chewing-gum bubble attacked his face. Since then, all he can talk about is how dangerous bubbles are.

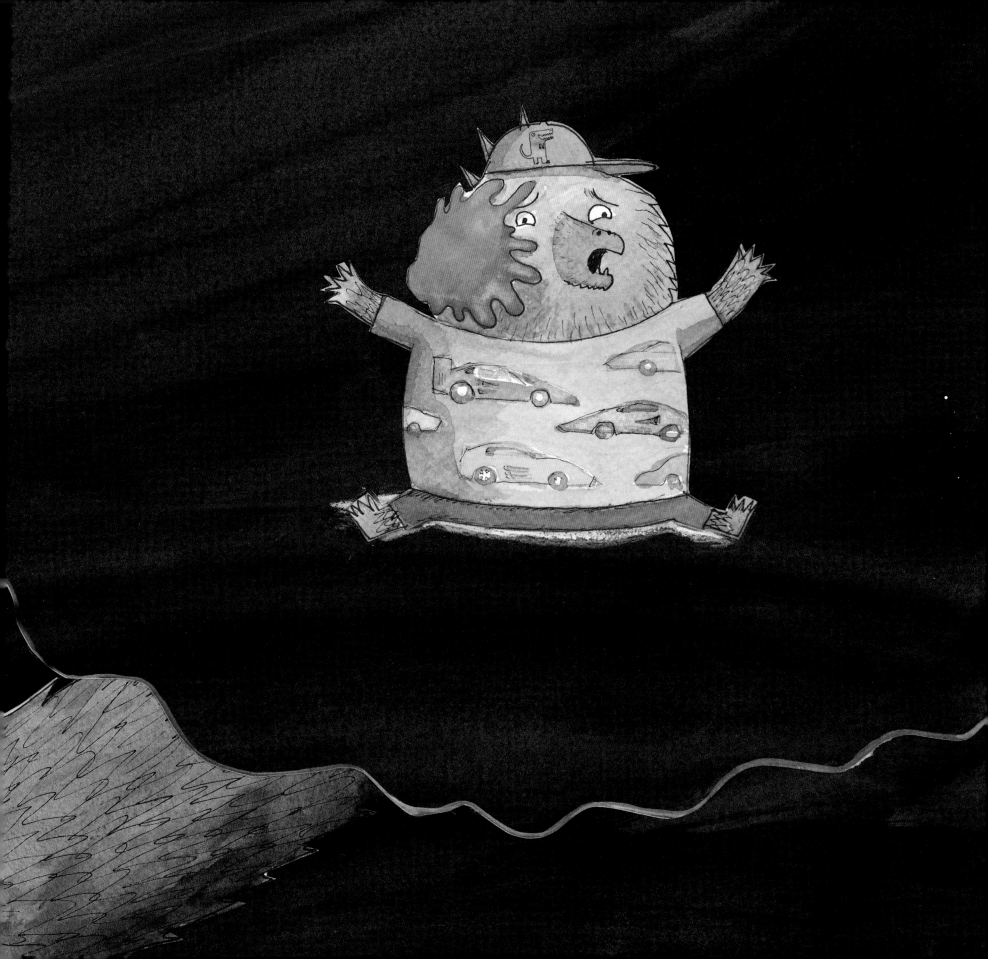

Bubbles are sneaky. You never hear them coming.

Where there's one bubble, there are many bubbles. They travel in packs.

Summer is the worst time for bubbles. That's when they go into a feeding frenzy.

Don't listen to Mogo. He has no idea what he's talking about.

I'll admit it's a bit surprising when a bubble suddenly appears out of nowhere. But that's part of the deal with living in La La Land. On the plus side, doughnuts grow on trees, and the rent is cheap.

FOR RENT
$26 per month

Hey, look! Here comes a bubble now.
Yerburt, stop running around in circles.
You have giant fangs.

Froofle, climb down from that tree.
Look at your claws. You have pointy claws.

Wumpus, get out from under those covers.
You're much too big for that bed anyhow.

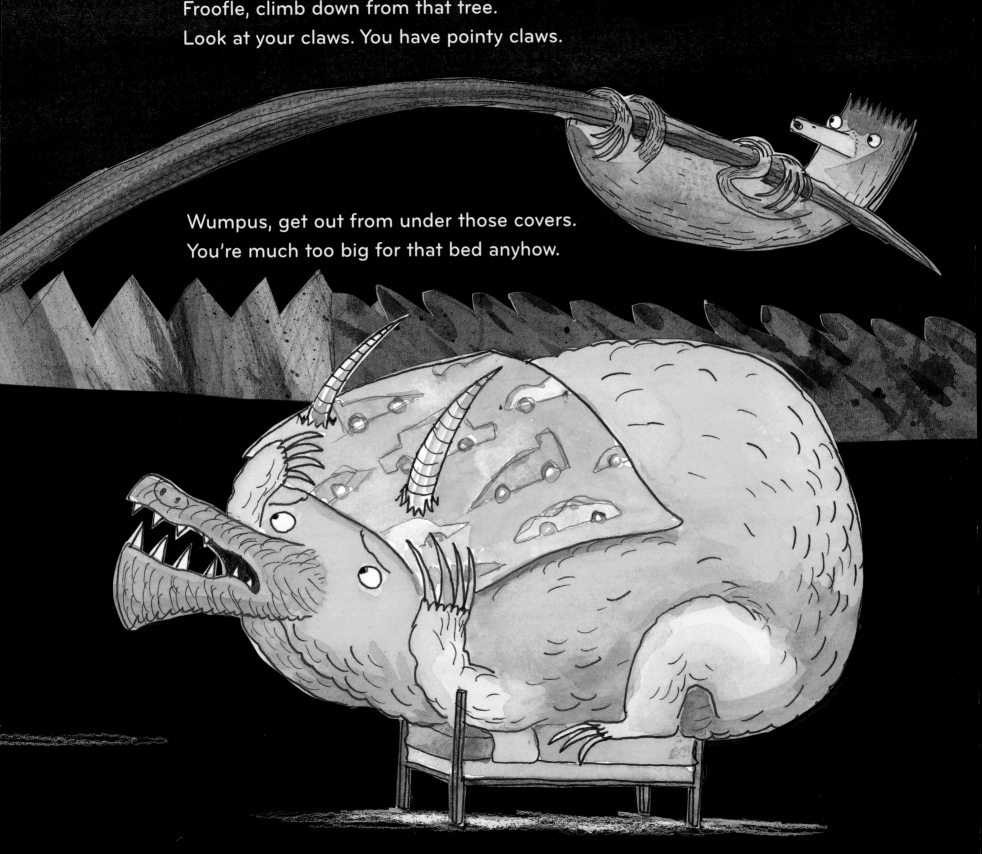

Look, here's a bubble. It's just a thin layer of
soap and water wrapped around a ball of air.
It's soft and delicate. It couldn't hurt a fly.

You could pop it with a little finger.

See?

Yerburt, use your fangs.

Yoofie, use your claws.

Wumpus, don't be scared. It's just a teeny, tiny . . . oh, wait. That's kind of a big one.

Wumpus. You can do it.

(Tell Wumpus he can do it.)

KABOOM!

See? Mogo doesn't know what he's talking about. There's no reason to be afraid.

Enjoy your bubble gum, Yerburt.

Have fun popping your bubble wrap, Froofle.

Oh, boy, that is a big bath full of bubbles, Wumpus!
(Tell Wumpus to save some water for the fish.)